A TALE OF
TWO TURKEYS

by Ellen Jackson
illustrated by Jenny Williams

WHISTLESTOP ®

Troll

Yoshka was the cleverest boy in the village of Askovitz. He knew some of this and some of that. But the lad longed to try his wits in the great world.

"My boy, it's a dog-eat-dog world out there," said Yoshka's father. "Such terrible stories I could tell you! Be content with your lot."

But Yoshka was not content.

One spring day a messenger arrived in the village of Askovitz with a proclamation.

"The czar of Russia has fallen ill," read the messenger. "Anyone who can cure him will receive 1,000 gold pieces. However, those who try and fail will receive three lashes each for wasting his Imperial Majesty's time."

Yoshka was excited, for here was a chance to test his cleverness.

The next day the boy left for St. Petersburg. When he arrived at the palace of the czar, he saw that a Cossack guarded an iron gate.

"I am here to cure the czar," said Yoshka to the Cossack. The Cossack looked Yoshka up and down.

"I will let you in," said the Cossack, "*if* you will agree to share one third of your reward with me."

Yoshka knew he had no choice, and so he agreed.

"To be sure you don't forget, we shall write down our agreement," said the shrewd Cossack.

He wrote a quick note, then opened the gate.

Yoshka strolled through the royal park. Soon he came upon a member of the Imperial Guards, standing before a bronze door.

"I am here to cure the czar," said Yoshka.

The guard looked Yoshka up and down.

"I will let you in," said the clever guard, "*if* you agree to give me one third of your reward."

Yoshka gulped. His share of the reward was disappearing fast. But what could he do? And so the guard wrote down the agreement, and Yoshka was allowed to enter.

After a short walk, Yoshka found himself before two huge doors of gold. He stepped up and pulled the bell.

The Grand Duke, a boy about the same age as Yoshka, stuck his head outside to see who it was.

"I am here to cure the czar," said Yoshka.

"I will let you in," said the Grand Duke, "*if* you promise to share one third of your reward."

What could poor Yoshka do? This was the last third of the reward and now he would have nothing left.

"Nevertheless, I will cure the czar and turn the tables on these scoundrels," thought Yoshka.

The Grand Duke wrote down their agreement, then allowed Yoshka to enter through the gates.

In the inner courtyard was a wooden table, and underneath the table was a large man in rags, scratching and pecking and making sounds like a bird.

"Who is that?" Yoshka whispered to the Grand Duke.

"That is my birdbrained papa, the czar," said the Grand Duke. "He thinks he is a turkey. That is his illness. It is great fun to play pranks on him, however. Yesterday, I put a rotten egg on the throne and told everyone that my papa had laid it."

Then he laughed like a fiend.

"Hmmmm," said Yoshka. "I need some time to think about this."

Yoshka thought and thought, and soon an idea came to him. In a moment he was under the table with the czar, scratching and pecking.

In silence the two of them scratched and pecked and scratched and pecked. After quite a while the czar said to Yoshka, "Who are you?"

"I am a turkey," said Yoshka, pecking at a bread crumb.

"What a coincidence!" said the czar. "So am I!"

So Yoshka and the czar scratched and pecked and pecked and scratched all day until night fell. Then they both went to the hen house to roost with the other turkeys.

The next morning the czar and Yoshka were up at dawn scratching and pecking, pecking and scratching. After about an hour, Yoshka said to the czar, "You know, I've been thinking. Why can't turkeys, such as ourselves, wear nice clothes instead of rags?"

"Why not indeed?" said the czar.

Yoshka summoned the czarina.

"Bring us fine clothes—fit for two turkeys!" he said.

The czarina brought fine clothes, and the czar and Yoshka put them on. Then they continued pecking and scratching.

The next day, when Yoshka and the czar were watching the czarina and the Grand Duke eat a magnificent feast, Yoshka said, "You know, I've been thinking. I don't see why turkeys, such as ourselves, cannot have a good meal now and then. Does eating real food make one less of a turkey?"

"Absolutely not," said the czar with a cluck.

Yoshka summoned the czarina once again.

"Bring us fine food—fit for two turkeys," he said.

And thus it was that Yoshka and the czar enjoyed their first meal at the table instead of under it.

That night in the hen house Yoshka's legs were stiff and tired from spending two days under the table.

"You know, I've been thinking," said Yoshka. "Why can't turkeys, such as ourselves, sleep in a real bed with pillows and a quilt? Don't turkeys deserve the finer things in life?"

"They certainly do!" said the czar, who had been trying to sleep like a turkey with his head under a wing.

Yoshka summoned the czarina once more.
"We need soft beds—fit for two turkeys," he said.
"Two roasting pans would do for the likes of you," said the Grand Duke with a sneer.
But Yoshka and the czar were taken to the palace where they were given two beds in which to sleep.

In this way, little by little as the days went by, the czar got better and better. Soon he was sitting on his throne and taking up his duties once again.

"It is time to collect my reward," thought Yoshka, who was very happy with his cleverness. That evening he went to see the czarina to ask for the 1,000 gold pieces.

But it was the czar as well as the czarina who greeted Yoshka in the great reception hall.

"I have learned much from you, my feathered friend," said the czar to Yoshka, "and I've been thinking. Why should a turkey, such as myself, have to listen to the cackling of barnyard birds, such as yourself? I much prefer royal company. Guards! Throw him out!"

"It is too bad after all your work," whispered the czarina to Yoshka. "But as you can see, although he has taken up his duties, in his mind he is still a turkey. I cannot say that he is cured."

"Don't forget the three lashes," said the Grand Duke, chuckling. "The law says that must be his reward."

"Why, silly me," said Yoshka. "Did you say reward? I almost forgot. That reward isn't mine to take. The Cossack, the guard, and the Grand Duke must split it between them."

Yoshka pulled the three notes out of his pocket and showed them to the czarina.

The czarina laughed. "You are a clever boy. I hope they appreciate your generosity."

So the Cossack and the guard received their fair share of the reward while Yoshka watched.

"And as for you . . . ," said the czarina, grabbing the arm of the Grand Duke.

"Unhand me, mother," said the Grand Duke. "No one can punish His Most Exalted Excellency, the Grand Duke!"

"No one except his Exalted Father, the czar," said Yoshka slyly. "Too bad he isn't here to give the boy his due. Alas, all I see is a royal turkey."

Everyone looked at the czar, who drew himself up to his full, regal height.

"Ahem!" said the czar. "Reward or no reward, that boy. . . that boy must get his comeuppance! And if the czar is the only one who can do it, then, very well—I am the czar!"

And so it was that the Grand Duke got his just desserts . . .

as did Yoshka.